To my godson Ayotunde

JANETTA OTTER-BARRY BOOKS

Text and illustrations copyright © Polly Alakija 2014
The right of Polly Alakija to be identified as the author and illustrator
of this work has been asserted by her in accordance with the Copyright,
Designs and Patents Act, 1988 (United Kingdom).

First published in Great Britain and in the USA in 2014 by
Frances Lincoln Children's Books, 74-77 White Lion Street, London N1 9PF
www.franceslincoln.com

A catalogue record for this book is available from the British Library.

ISBN 978-1-84780-437-2

Illustrated with acrylic and pencils

Set in Jenson Pro

Printed in China

3 5 7 9 8 6 4 2

COUNTING CHICKENS

POLLY ALAKIJA

F

FRANCES LINCOLN
CHILDREN'S BOOKS

Tobi was the proud owner
of the finest hen in his village.

Tobi's friends all had their own animals too.

On Monday, Ade's cow had a calf.

Tobi's hen laid one egg.

On Tuesday, Tunde's sheep had two lambs.

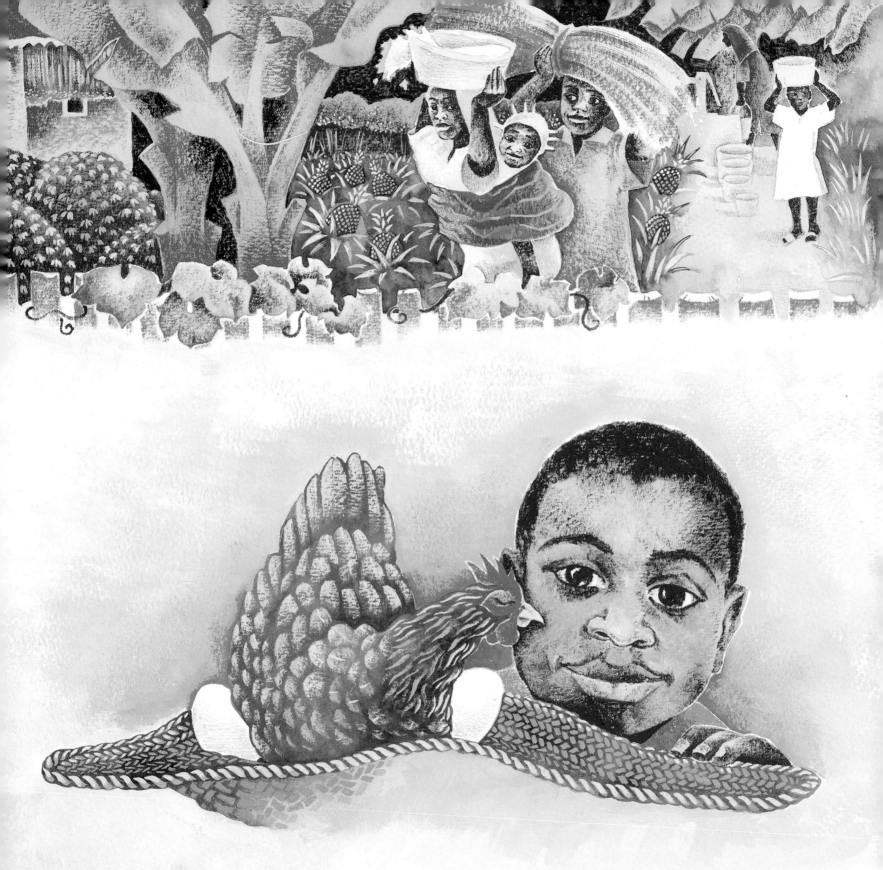

Tobi's hen laid a second egg.

On Wednesday, Bisi's goat had three kids.

Tobi's hen laid a third egg.

On Thursday, Aduke's cat had four kittens.

Tobi's hen laid a fourth egg.

On Friday, Laolu's dog had five puppies.

Tobi's hen laid a fifth egg.

On Saturday, Dapo's pig had six piglets.

Tobi's hen laid a sixth egg.

On Sunday, Tobi's hen
laid a seventh egg.
And there they sat, waiting.

One week later, Ade's calf mooed loudly.
Tunde's lambs could run and skip.
Bisi's kids climbed about.

BUT...
Tobi sat with his hen,
waiting.

Two weeks later,
Aduke's kittens chased their tails.
Laolu's puppies chased the kittens.
Dapo's piglets rolled in the dust.

BUT...
Tobi sat with his hen,
waiting.

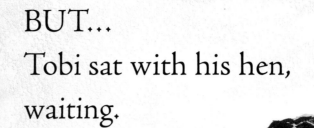

Tobi's friends teased him and said
that they would eat his eggs for breakfast.

But then...

after twenty-one days,
Tobi was waiting no more.

And neither was his fine hen.
They both watched, with great pride,
as their brood of seven beautiful chicks hatched.

Soon, the seven chicks grew into hens,
almost as perfect as their mother hen.
The next year they all had chicks of their own.

Now Tobi is the proud owner
of so many chickens he can't
count them all.

Can you?

There are 50 chickens.